# The Cricket Boy

**and**
**Other Stories**

## CONTENTS

**STECK-VAUGHN**
C O M P A N Y

# A Strange New Friend

He sat in the corner just staring at me,
His eyes bright and shining and red as can be.
He had long pointed fingers and a green scaly skin,
And it gave me the shivers just looking at him.

But then I looked closer and to my surprise,
I noticed the monster had tears in his eyes.
He looked at me sadly and started to speak,
And the tears fell like rain down his green scaly cheek.

"Oh please don't be frightened," he sobbed through his
    tears,
"I've wanted a playmate for so many years,
And then when I saw you this bright sunny day,
I hoped and I hoped that you wanted to play."

So, I sat down beside him and took his green hand.
I'd made a new friend and the feeling was grand.
It's not what one looks like that counts in the end,
The real thing that matters is having a friend.

Peggy Clulow

# The Cricket Boy

Long ago in the far away land of China
there lived a man called Hu.
He didn't like to work hard in the fields all day.
He just liked asking questions.
But to find the answers he had to think and
he had to read books.
Hu would ask,
    "Why do small things grow big?"
    "Why is the sun hot?"
    "Why does the spring come after winter?"
All the people in the village thought he was very clever.

Hu had a son called Chang.
Chang did not like asking questions.
He didn't like thinking or reading.
What he liked best was to play with his crickets.
Hu was sad that his son didn't like asking questions.
So he said to himself, "If Chang doesn't want to learn
to like books, then I must learn to like crickets."
So Hu would sit with Chang and together
they would watch the crickets.
Soon Hu began to wonder, "Why do some crickets sing
more loudly than others?"

Then he said,
  "Why are some crickets so small?"
  "Why are some crickets such brave fighters?"
And together Hu and Chang would watch
and talk and learn.
Soon they found a favorite cricket.
He was the best fighter of all.
Chang called him Black Dragon.
Chang's friends also had crickets.
Sometimes the boys would have cricket fights.
Black Dragon always won.
He was famous.

    One day an important man came riding into
the village on a white horse.

    "Where is Chang?" he asked. "The Emperor of China
wants to see him. He wants to see Black Dragon fight."
Chang was very excited.

    So Hu and Chang packed their bags and
got ready to leave the very next day.
When everything was ready, Chang went to his room
to get Black Dragon.

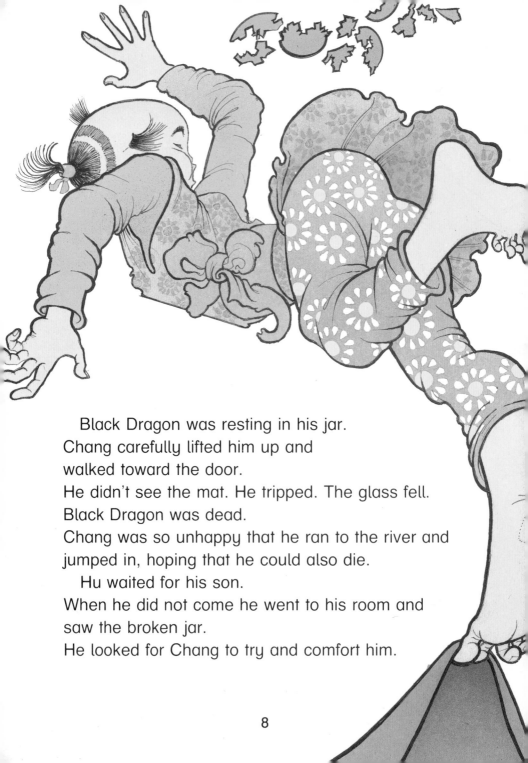

Black Dragon was resting in his jar.
Chang carefully lifted him up and
walked toward the door.
He didn't see the mat. He tripped. The glass fell.
Black Dragon was dead.
Chang was so unhappy that he ran to the river and
jumped in, hoping that he could also die.
    Hu waited for his son.
When he did not come he went to his room and
saw the broken jar.
He looked for Chang to try and comfort him.

Just then a fisherman came to the house.

"Look, Hu," he called, "I have found your son. He was in the river. He looks very ill."

Then Hu was very unhappy.

He quickly put Chang on the bed.

He thought his son was dead. He began to pray.

As he prayed a voice said to him, "Go to the gate and look behind the big stone."

Hu did as the voice told him.

There behind the big stone was a small cricket.

Gently he lifted it up in his hand.

"This must be a sign. I must take this cricket to the emperor. I shall call it Bright Dragon."

When the emperor saw Hu's small cricket,
he laughed.

"How can a small cricket like that be a great fighter?"
he asked.

Then the fights began. Bright Dragon won every fight.
After ten fights the emperor said, "I give up.
Your little cricket is so brave he wins every time.
What would you like for a prize?"

Hu hung his head.

"There is only one thing I want," he said, "but you cannot give it to me."

The emperor was very surprised.

"What is that?" he asked.

"All I want is for my son to be well again," said Hu.

"In that case you must go home at once," said the emperor. "Go and look after him. I will give you some medicine to make him better."

So Hu started the long journey back again.
As soon as he was home, he ran to his son's bed.
Chang lay quite still.

"My son," cried Hu. "Can you hear me?
Our little cricket won. He won every match.
The emperor has sent you some medicine."
Just then Chang opened his eyes.
He looked at his father.

"Father," he said, "I had such a strange dream.
I dreamt that I had to fight the great emperor himself.
We fought ten times and I won every time.
Then the emperor turned to me and said,
'You are so brave that you can go home now.'
Now I feel better, I shall get up."

That night there was a party for the whole village.
Hu was so glad that his son was well again.
Everyone wanted to hear the story of the emperor and
how Bright Dragon had won the fight.

When everyone had at last gone to sleep,
Hu sat down and looked at the stars.
He wondered, "Why are they shining so brightly?
How did the little cricket win?
What really happened to Chang?"

But I don't think that he will ever know
the answers to those questions.
Do you?

# That Jimbo

    Jimbo the dog lived with Mr. and Mrs. Jones and their children, Sue and Sam.
Jimbo was a little dog.
He had large floppy ears and a curly brown coat.
He always smiled happily and wagged his tail.
    "This is my family. I am very happy," barked Jimbo.

He rolled in the grass. He chased cats.
He barked at other dogs. He ran along the river bank.
He visited the people next door.
He played with the children in the street.
He even swam in the goldfish pond!
　　"You are a bad dog, Jimbo," said Sue.
　　"You are a nice dog, Jimbo," said Sam.
Jimbo jumped up and licked his face.
They all had fun together.

During the summer, Anna came to stay.
Sue and Sam were her cousins.
Anna lived in another town far away.
She came in a plane by herself.
She was six years old.
Mr. and Mrs. Jones and Sue and Sam went to
the airport to meet her.
Jimbo stayed at home.

"How nice to see you, Anna," said her aunt.
She gave her a big hug. So did her uncle.

"We'll get your suitcase," said Sue and Sam.
They liked having Anna visit.

"When we get home, you can play with Jimbo,"
said Sue.

Jimbo? Anna stood still.
She had forgotten that her cousins had a dog.

Anna was afraid of dogs.
Dogs looked big and fierce. She did not like dogs.
She loved Toto, her cat. She loved Tom, her bird.
But she was not sure that she would love Jimbo.
Anna was very quiet on the way home from
the airport.
Soon they arrived at Sam and Sue's house.

Jimbo was very pleased to see his family again.
He shook with delight. His ears stood up stiffly.
A big welcoming grin was on his face.

"Here they come," he said to himself.
"I will give them my loudest bark. **Woof, woof**."

Anna did not like Jimbo's bark at all.

"Oh dear," she thought. "That Jimbo sounds very fierce."

"Everyone get out of the car," called her uncle. "We're home."

Jimbo jumped up at the car window.

Anna looked at him as she got out of the car and walked inside with her uncle.

"That girl has brown eyes just like mine," thought Jimbo.

He loved Anna from that moment.

"Don't be afraid of Jimbo," said her aunt to Anna. "He likes you. Really he does."

Anna felt safe once she was in the house.
But poor Jimbo was sad.
His ears drooped. He wagged his tail slowly.
He wanted Anna to play with him.
He wanted her to be his special friend.

The next day Sue and Sam went outside
to play with Anna.
Jimbo was very happy to see them.
He ran around. He jumped up and down.
Anna tried hard not to be afraid.
She stayed close to Sam and Sue.

Jimbo is nice in so many ways, thought
Anna to herself.
He is always smiling. He has lovely brown hair.
He has big brown eyes. He is very friendly.
But he seems so big.
He wants to jump up and lick my face and
he barks very loudly.

Sam ran to the back door and took down
Jimbo's leash from its hook.

"Come on, Anna," he said cheerfully.
"I'm taking Jimbo for a walk.
We will take him on his leash.
He won't jump up. He won't bark."

Anna held Sam's hand very tightly.
They all walked down the street.
Jimbo thought happily, "I like going for
walks with Anna and Sam."

"Would you like to hold Jimbo's leash?"
Sam asked Anna.
"I will hold your hand. Don't be afraid."
    So Anna held Sam's hand and with her
other hand she held Jimbo's leash.
She felt very brave.
Suddenly she also felt happy.
    Jimbo also felt happy.
He thought, "I will turn around and thank Anna
for being my friend."

As they walked along he suddenly stopped and
looked back at Anna.

"Thank you, Anna," he barked. "Woof, woof."
Anna was frightened.
Sam had to stop her from running away.

"Never mind, Anna," he said.
"You will soon like Jimbo."

They went home and the children went
inside for lunch.
Jimbo trotted away. He was feeling happy.
He had enjoyed his walk with Anna and Sam.
He felt like running and jumping.
He raced around the house. He chased the cat.
He picked up a stick in his sharp teeth.
He ran around and around with it.

Suddenly he saw a big box on the grass.

"I will jump over that box," he thought.

Too late!

The stick caught on the box as he jumped.

His back leg hit the box. A pain shot through it.

Poor Jimbo. He limped to the front door.

"Help me! I have hurt myself," he barked.

Nobody heard him. Nobody came.

Anna finished her lunch.

"May I go outside and play?" she asked.

"Of course you may," said her aunt.

Anna ran out the front door.

She did not know that Jimbo was there.

"Oh," she cried. Then she stopped.

What was wrong with Jimbo?

Jimbo was not barking. Jimbo was not jumping.

Anna saw that Jimbo was limping.

Suddenly Anna was not afraid of Jimbo.

"Jimbo," she said, and she bent down by
the dog. "Don't worry, Jimbo," she whispered.
"I'll go and get help."

"Aunt, aunt," she called. "Jimbo has hurt his leg.
Please come quickly."

Everyone ran outside.

Her aunt picked up Jimbo very carefully.

Her uncle drove them all in the car to see the vet.

The vet felt Jimbo's leg gently.

"He has hurt a muscle," he said. "I will put
a bandage on it."

"I'm glad Jimbo is not badly hurt," said Anna.

"So are we," said Sue and Sam.

"So are we," said her aunt and uncle.

Jimbo was taken care of until his leg
was strong again.
Who took care of Jimbo?
Who was the happiest when Jimbo was better?
Why, Anna of course.